Betsey Biggalow has more surprises in store.

Ten funny, warm stories about this lovable young miss who is full of bright ideas that don't usually turn out the way she expected . . . or wanted!

Laugh with Betsey as she puts on a show, stars on the telly, finds out that she can win a race without a secret weapon and that moving house is really quite nice. Be serious with Betsey when she has a HELP THE WORLD DAY, becomes as fierce as a guard dog and learns to put her best-friend before herself. Share Betsey's fun-filled days in the West Indies as she rides a bike, goes to the market and best of all, when Dad comes home.

OTHER BOOKS
BY MALORIE BLACKMAN

Jack Sweettooth the 73rd
Puffin

Snow Dog
Transworld

The Monster Crisp Guzzler
Transworld

Ellie and the Cat
Green Apple

Whizziwig & Whizziwig Returns
Puffin

The Big Book of Betsey Biggalow
Barn Owl

The Amazing Adventures of Girl Wonder
Barn Owl

MALORIE BLACKMAN

The
BUMPER
BOOK
of
Betsey
Biggalow

Illustrated by Patrice Aggs

Barn Owl Books

Meet Betsey Biggalow

– a lively young lady
who knows her own mind!

and . . .

... her family

Mam

Dad

Gran'ma Liz

Desmond
(Betsey's brother)

Sherena
(Betsey's sister)

... and friends

May

Prince
(Betsey's dog)

Josh

To Neil and Lizzy, with love

BARN OWL BOOKS

157 Fortis Green Road, London, N10 3LX

This selection and arrangement
published by Barn Owl Books, 2007
157 Fortis Green Road, London, N10 3LX

Distributed by Frances Lincoln,
4 Torriano Mews, Torriano Avenue, London, NW5 2RZ

Stories first published in the following books:
Betsey Biggalow is here! - 1992
Betsey Biggalow The Detective - 1992
Hurricane Betsey - 1993
Magic Betsey - 1994
Betsey's Birthday Surprise - 1996

ISBN 978 190301577 3

Front cover photography (girl) © Hola Images/Getty
Front cover photography (background) © Tony Hamer
Designed and typeset by Skandesign Limited
Printed in the UK by Cox and Wyman

Contents

1

The Best Show in the World

Betsey stretched her hands out in
front of her, before resting them on
the keyboard.

    'I'm now going to make up a
song off the top of my head and
play it for you,' said Betsey very
importantly. Then she plonked her

hands up and down the keyboard running them over the black and white keys.

'Betsey, no more – please,' Sherena begged. 'You are driving me up the wall, round the twist, off my head! That noise your making is *horrible*!'

'It's not noise. It's music!' said Betsey and she started playing again.

'My name is Betsey,
And I live in a house.
I don't have a cat,
And I don't have a mouse!
Yeah! Yeah! Yeah!'

It sounded good to her!

Prince, the family black and brown Alsatian dog, raised his head and began to howl.

'Hoooo! Owww-owww!' yowled Prince.

'Betsey, I'll give you anything you want if you'll just hush up!' pleaded Desmond. 'Look, you're even getting on Prince's nerves now!'

'Botheration, Desmond! You don't know good music when you hear it,' frowned Betsey. 'And I'm not getting on Prince's nerves. He's singing along with me.'

PLONK! PLINK! PLONK! Betsey banged on the keyboard even louder than before. Playing the keyboard was such fun! The music sounded really good – and the louder she played, the better it sounded! Dad had bought the keyboard for all of them, before he'd had to leave for another year of studying. Dad was going to be a doctor.

Just then the front door opened and in walked Mam and Gran'ma Liz.

'Mam, make her stop! Please make her stop!' wailed Sherena.

'She's driving us bonkers!' Desmond moaned, his hands over his ears.

'Look Mam! Listen Gran'ma Liz! I've made up a song,' said Betsey. She ran her fingers up and down the keyboard.

'My name is Betsey,
And I live in a house.
I don't have a cat,

And I don't have a mouse!
Yeah! Yeah! Yeah!'

'Isn't that brilliant!' Betsey asked.

'It's very good, Betsey.' Mam started to shake her head, then quickly turned it into a nod.

'Lovely, child,' said Gran'ma Liz, weakly. 'But don't you think the

keyboard should have a rest now?'

'Oh no, Gran'ma. This keyboard is the best present in the world and it's going to last forever and ever,' said Betsey. "Besides, I need to practise.'

'Why?' asked Mam.

'May and I are going to put on a show for all of you,' announced Betsey. 'It's going to be the best show in the whole world.'

'Oh-oh!' Sherena muttered.

'I don't like the sound of that,' Desmond mumbled.

'Betsey, I think you should have asked us first,' said Mam.

'Why' asked Betsey.

'Because . . . because . . .' But Mam couldn't think of a single reason!

For the next few days, May came over in the afternoons after school. May and Betsey sat in front of the keyboard giggling and playing music – at least that's what they both called it!

The next day was Saturday. Mam invited some of her friends and neighbours over and soon there were grown-ups in almost every part of the sitting-room. But to Mam and Gran'ma Liz's surprise, other people started arriving at the house as well. First there was May, then came Josh and Celeste and others from Betsey's class.

'You're all welcome but what's going on?' asked Mam.

'We've come to see Betsey's show,' Josh replied.

'Betsey's show!' Mam's eyes opened like saucers. Mam turned to look at Betsey. 'Elizabeth Ruby Biggalow, I want a word with you in your room.'

Ooops! Whenever Mam used Betsey's whole, full name then Betsey knew she was in for some serious talking!

'Why didn't you tell me that you'd invited all your friends over to hear your show?' Mam asked. 'And why didn't you tell me you were putting on your show *today*?'

'Sorry, Mam,' said Betsey. 'I thought it would be fun to put on a show for the grown-ups as well, as a sort of surprise.'

'Did you? Well, you should have told me first,' said Mam.

'Your friends will like it, Mam,' smiled Betsey. 'It's going to be the best show in the world.'

'Hhmm!' was all Mam said.

Betsey walked back to the keyboard. 'Are you ready?' she whispered to May.

May swallowed hard, then nodded. 'I think so.'

Betsey stood up. 'Ladies and gentlemen,' she began grandly. 'Please take your seats. May and I are going to put on a show for you. We've been practising and practising.'

'I'm off! I'm going to my friend Marlon's house,' said Desmond.

'You can't go now,' said Betsey. 'Please, we're just about to start. Mam, tell him!'

'Desmond, wait until your sister's show is over,' said Mam.

'Do I have to?' groaned Desmond.

'Give her a chance,' Mam replied.

'Desmond, you'll like it honest!' said Betsey.

Desmond muttered something under his breath. It sounded like 'Bet I don't!' but it could have been 'No, I won't!'

May and Betsey sat next to each other and placed their hands on the keys. Betsey slid the volume control up to maximum.

'This song is called *The Sing-Along Song*! Ready, everyone?' Betsey asked.

They all nodded. Betsey and May plonked their hands down on the keyboard and began to run their fingers up and down the keys. Then they both started to sing:

'We're May and Betsey
And we made up this song.
And with this song,
We can't go wrong!
This song is big,
This song is strong.
This song is a Sing-Along song!'

'This song is very, *very* long,' whispered Sherena.

'Shush!' hissed Mam.

Betsey and May carried on singing.

'*So if you really like this song,*
Take a breath and sing-along.'

Betsey and May started singing their song from the beginning and playing the keyboard at the same time. All their friends started singing first, while the grown-ups just looked at each other. Then something very strange happened.

Mam started it. She started singing along too! The Gran'ma Liz joined in, saying, 'If you can't beat 'em, join 'em.' Sherena and Desmond looked around the room in amazement. All the other grown-ups were singing as well, huge, great grins

on their faces.

'Oh well!' said Sherena. And with a laugh, both Desmond and Sherena started singing too. Desmond and Sherena gave out biscuits and cake and everyone had a lot of fun!

Later that day, Gran'ma Liz

said, 'Well done, Betsey. I *did* enjoy your show. I haven't laughed so much in a long, long time.'

'I told you you'd enjoy it,' said Betsey. 'I told you it would be the best show in the world. And what's more, we're going to put on lots and lots more shows . . . We're going to put a show on every week from now on . . .'

'Mam!' Desmond and Sherena squealed.

'Quite right!' smiled Mam. 'In fact Betsey, I've been talking it over with Gran'ma Liz and we both think that as you're so keen, we'll find the money to send you to piano lessons with Mrs Paul from the other side of town. You can have one lesson every two weeks and practise every day. When you've learnt a few more songs, then you can put on another show.'

'Lessons?' Betsey's jaw dropped. 'Did you say lessons?'

'I certainly did,' said Mam.

'Oh . . . lessons?' Betsey didn't sound too keen.

'Don't you want to learn to play the keyboard properly?' asked Mam.

'I guess so. But lessons . . . Er, Mam, can I have a think about it?' asked Betsey.

'Of course you can. Take all the time you need,' smiled Mam.

Funny, but that was the last time Betsey even touched the keyboard for a long, long while!

2

Betsey Biggalow is here

Betsey Biggalow had another of her
bright and shiny ideas! Today would
be her HELP THE WORLD day! The
question was, who should she help
first? She ran into the sitting-room.
Sherena was sitting at the table,
books, books and more books spread

out in front of her.

'Have no fear! Betsey Biggalow is here!' said Betsey proudly.

'Not now, Betsey. Can't you see I'm busy?' said Sherena.

Betsey walked across to peer over her sister's shoulder.

'What are you doing?'

Sherena looked up, annoyed. 'I'm trying to *revise* for my Maths test on Monday.'

'I'll help you,' Betsey insisted.

'You can help me by disappearing,' Sherena said crossly. 'Go on! Vanish! Depart! Leave! Go away!'

'All right. You don't have to go on,' said Betsey. 'If you don't need my help, I'll go and find someone who does.'

'You do that!' said Sherena, her head buried back in the book in front of her.

Betsey ran out into the backyard to see her brother. Desmond was seeding the fowls which clucked and

pecked and pecked and clucked.

'Have no fear! Betsey Biggalow is here!' said Betsey. 'I've come to help.'

'I don't need the help of a shrimp like you,' Desmond scoffed. 'Besides, how come you wait till I've almost finished before coming to help me?'

'Well, I'm here now,' said Betsey. Helping the world was turning out to be more difficult than she'd ever imagined.

'Betsey Biggalow, what are you up to?' Gran'ma Liz came out into the yard. 'If you're seeking useful employment, I can soon find a hundred and one things for you to do.'

Betsey shuddered. She was looking for one interesting something to do – not a hundred and one boring somethings!

'No thanks, Gran'ma Liz' said Betsey. 'I was just about to go and see my friend May.'

'Hhmm!' said Gran'ma Liz. 'Well, just make sure you're back before supper.'

Betsey didn't need to be told twice. It was time to scarper before Gran'ma Liz decided that her one hundred and one things should come before a visit to May.

So off Betsey went, down the track, along the road, to May's house. The evening sun was still hot, hot, hot and the sugar cane in the fields on either side of the road, cast long, evening shadows.

'Botheration! So much for "Have no fear, Betsey Biggalow is here!"' Betsey muttered with disgust.

And so much for helping the world. You just couldn't help the world when it didn't want your help. Betsey was so deep in thought that she almost didn't hear it. She stopped, and frowned and looked around. Then it came again.

'Help . . . oh please help me . . .'

Frightened, Betsey looked around. 'Who's that? Who's there?'

'Over here . . ' the faint voice said.

Slowly, oh so slowly and oh so carefully, Betsey crept towards the voice. Then she saw him. There, lying

in a ditch by the side of the road, was
a man with a moustache. He was
lying half on his side, half on his back.
And there, on top of his left leg, was a
motorbike.

    'I . . . I think I've broken my leg,'
the man whispered. Betsey could see
the perspiration all over his cheeks and
his chin. His wet face glistened in the
evening sunshine. His shirt was damp
and sticking to him just as closely as
Gran'ma Liz's Sunday hat stuck to
her head.

'Wait . . . wait there. I'll go and get my gran'ma,' Betsey said. 'I'll be right back.'

'What's your . . . your name . . .' asked the man.

'Betsey. Betsey Biggalow.'

'Hurry Betsey . . .' the man gasped, before his eyes closed and his head nodded down towards the ground.

Betsey ran. She raced like the wind.

'Gran'ma Liz! Gran'ma Liz! There's a man. And he's broken his leg. And he's lying in a ditch. And his motorbike is lying on his leg. And his eyes are closed. And . . .'

'Calm down, child,' frowned

Gran'ma Liz. 'Now what're you saying?'

So Betsey explained all over again. The words fell over each other, each one in a rush to be heard. Desmond came in from the garden and Sherena left her books in the sitting-room to listen. By the time Betsey had finished explaining she was out of breath.

'You'd better take us to him,' Gran'ma Liz got a blanket and off they all went. At last they reached the part of the road where Betsey had seen the man and his motorbike in the ditch. And he was still there, his eyes closed, his body as still as Sunday morning.

'Sherena, run back to the house and 'phone for an ambulance. Desmond, Betsey, help me move this motorbike off his leg.' Gran'ma Liz got busy at once.

'Is he all right?' Desmond puffed as they tried to shift the motorbike.

'He's still breathing and that's something,' said Gran'ma Liz. 'He's unconscious. The pain was probably too much.'

'Should we move him?' asked Betsey.

'No. When someone's been in a road accident you shouldn't move them. The ambulance men will know how to move him the right way,' Gran'ma Liz said. 'I'll cover him with

this blanket I brought with me.'

'Why does he need a blanket? It's hot-baking!' said Betsey.

'Anyone who's had a shock should be kept warm. You can get cold very quickly when you've had a serious accident. We'll stand and watch over him until the ambulance arrives.'

'Look, Gran'ma Liz. The front tyre of his bike is flat.' Desmond pointed. 'He must have got a puncture and skidded off the road.'

'If the good Lord had meant for us to go tearing around to up, down, below and above, we would have petrol in our bodies, not blood,' Gran'ma Liz sniffed. Gran'ma Liz didn't approve of cars and motorbikes.

After a long, short time, the ambulance finally arrived, its lights flashing, its siren wailing. Betsey watched, holding her breath, as the ambulance men lifted the man with the broken leg onto a stretcher. The injured man's eyes fluttered open and saw Betsey.

'It's okay. You're going to the hospital now,' said Betsey.

'Thank you, Betsey,' smiled the man. 'I'm going to be fine now.' And he closed his eyes as he was carried over to the ambulance. In only a few moments, the ambulance went roaring away towards the hospital, its siren wailing.

'Will the man and his leg be all right?' asked Betsey.

'He'll be fine. At the hospital they'll fix him up in no time,' smiled Gran'ma Liz. 'Betsey, you did very well. You were right to come and get me.'

Betsey thought hard for a moment.

'I didn't help the whole world today,' she said. 'But I did help a little bit of it. I think that's okay.'

'Of course it's okay. I'm proud of you, Betsey,' said Gran'ma Liz.

And what did Betsey do? Betsey just smiled.

3

Betsey and the Secret Weapon

'Go, Betsey! Go!'

Betsey ran as fast as she could – but it wasn't fast enough. Her best friend May flashed past her on the right. Josh whizzed by her on the left.

'Run, Betsey!'

Betsey could hear her bigger brother Desmond shouting to her.

She tried to run faster but Josh and
May and Ce-Ce were now way out in
front. Betsey slowed down. She'd never
catch them now.

'BETSEY, RUN!' Desmond
yelled.

Betsey didn't stop but she didn't
run flat out either. What was the
point? She'd never catch up with her
friends now.

Betsey finished the race last.
Desmond walked over to her and put

his arm around her shoulders.

'Never mind, Betsey. You'll do better next time.'

'No I won't,' Betsey sniffed. 'I'm a useless runner. Everyone always beats me. I bet even Gran'ma Liz could beat me!'

'I don't think so!' Desmond smiled.

'Yes, she could,' Betsey insisted.

'It was only a practice run,' Desmond pointed out. 'The real race

isn't until next Friday. That gives you plenty of time to get better.'

'I'm not going to run any more stupid races,' Betsey kicked at the sand, her head bent.

May jogged over, puffing as she ran.

'Bad luck, Betsey. Better luck next time,' smiled May.

'May, don't be such a show-off!' Betsey fumed. And off she marched.

'There's no need to bite my head off just 'cause you lost!' May called after her. 'Bad loser!'

Betsey ignored her and carried on walking home. She'd never, ever won a race. Her friends always beat her and she always came last or close

to it. She'd never be able to run.
Never. Never. Never.

Desmond ran up and started
walking beside her.

'Betsey, just do your best. That's
all that matters,' said Desmond.

'Botheration, Desmond, I *am*
doing my best, but it doesn't get me
anywhere – except last,' sniffed Betsey.

'It's only a race,' said Desmond.

'That's all right for you to say.
You've never come last in a running
race,' said Betsey miserably.

Desmond chewed on his bottom
lip and thought for a while.

'Betsey, if I tell you a secret, do
you promise never to tell anyone else?'
Desmond said at last.

Betsey stopped walking and looked up at her brother. He looked absolutely serious.

'I promise,' Betsey breathed.

It wasn't often that Desmond shared his secrets!

'I always used to come last in my races,' Desmond began. 'Until something strange, something really *peculiar* happened.'

'What was that?' Betsey asked.

'I found a secret weapon to help me with my running,' Desmond whispered.

'A secret weapon? What was it?' asked Betsey, her eyes as round as saucers.

'A pair of running shoes,' whispered Desmond.

'Is that all?' Betsey's shoulders slumped with disappointment.

'Ah, but they weren't just any old pair of running shoes. They were special. They were *magic*!'

'They were?'

Desmond nodded. 'Every time I wore those shoes I never lost a race.'

'Where are those shoes now?' Betsey asked.

'In a secret place,' winked Desmond.

'Oh Desmond, let me borrow them. Please!' Betsey begged.

Desmond studied Betsey closely.

'Only on one condition . . .' he said at last.

'Anything,' Betsey interrupted.

She would agree to anything if it meant she could borrow Desmond's secret weapon.

'You can't tell anyone about them,' said Desmond. 'It's got to be our secret or the magic might not work.'

'Agreed!' Betsey said at once.

'There's something else,' said Desmond. He pulled Betsey closer.

'What's that?' Betsey asked.

'I'll give you the shoes tonight, but you've got to practice running and running in them to get used to them. Then the shoes will know that they've got to transfer their magic from my feet to yours,' Desmond explained.

'I can do that,' said Betsey. 'I'll run in them every day until the race.'

'D'you promise?' said Desmond.

'I promise,' said Betsey.

She was going to use Desmond's secret weapon. She'd never lose another running race again!

Every day after that, Betsey ran!

She ran before school and during the break times at school and after school. She ran everywhere, all day, every day until Gran'ma Liz said, 'Betsey, if you're not careful, you'll run until there's nothing left of you but a greasy spot!'

Betsey didn't care. She carried on running!

At last Friday arrived – the school's sports day. It seemed like everyone in the district turned up. And Betsey's race was the next event. Betsey stood at the starting line with her other friends. But this time, she wasn't worried. Oh no! This time she had Desmond's secret weapon. She was wearing his magic running shoes. They didn't look like much of a secret weapon. They were old and tatty and the bits that should have been white were now grey. But that didn't matter. Betsey could feel their magic spinning up through her legs right to the top of her head.

Desmond came running over.

'Ready, Betsey?' Desmond winked.

'Ready,' Betsey smiled.

'Remember, you've got to really believe in their magic and run flat out. Run harder than you ever have before and *don't give up*,' said Desmond.

'Okay,' Betsey nodded.

She bent down and touched her secret weapons for luck.

Desmond ran back to the sidelines. Betsey waved at her whole family who had come to cheer her on. There was Mam, Gran'ma Liz and her bigger sister, Sherena as well as Desmond. Betsey sighed. It would've been wonderful if Dad could've been there as well, but he wasn't due home for another three weeks.

Betsey turned and looked down

the beach to the finish line. She ignored the birds singing in the coconut trees. She concentrated on the finishing line down the beach and nothing else.

'Are you ready?' the judge called out. 'On your marks . . . GO!'

Betsey raced like the wind. She didn't look to see where anyone else was. She didn't pause or slow down but she kept her eyes on the finishing line. And in no time at all she was running past it.

'Hooray! Hooray! Well done Betsey.'

Betsey looked around. Mam and Sherena and Desmond were running up to her, followed by Gran'ma Liz.

'Did I win? Did I win?' asked

Betsey. She wasn't sure.

'No. May came first – but you came second!' grinned Sherena.

Mam hugged Betsey tight. 'I'm so proud of you, Betsey. Well done!'

Second . . .

'I didn't come first . . . but second is a lot better than coming last all the time!' Betsey decided.

Betsey ran over to her friend, May.

'Well done, May!' said Betsey.

'Congratulations, Betsey,' said May. 'You almost caught me. I only just won!'

'Maybe next time I'll beat you,' said Betsey.

'Maybe . . . and maybe not!' said May.

Betsey laughed and ran back to her family. But then disaster struck! The sole of one of the trainers came unstuck and started flapping around under Betsey's foot like a bird's wing.

'Desmond look! Look at your secret weapon,' Betsey wailed. 'How will I ever win another race now?'

'Betsey . . . I've got a confession to make,' Desmond began. 'Those running shoes . . . they're not really a secret weapon. They're not really magic.'

'Yes, they are,' Betsey frowned. 'I wouldn't have come second if it wasn't for them.'

'That was *you*, Betsey, not the shoes. They're just my old running shoes. You came second because you practised and you didn't give up,' said Desmond.

Betsey looked down at the trainers. They didn't look so magic any more. They just looked old and battered.

'They're not magic . . . ?' Betsey asked.

Desmond shook his head.

Betsey slowly smiled. 'Well, if they're not magic, then it must be me. I'm the secret weapon!'

'Too right!' Desmond grinned.

'I'm going to keep practising and I'm going to get better and better at running,' Betsey smiled. 'And to be honest, Desmond, I'm glad these old running shoes aren't magic.'

'Why?' asked Desmond.

'Because that means that I can go back to wearing my own trainers again. I don't have to wear your ones any more,' Betsey said. 'Your trainers stink of pong-smelly cheese and there's nothing magic about that!'

Betsey and the Birthday Present

NEW!

'Mam! Gran'ma Liz!' Betsey burst
into the house and raced into the
kitchen.

'Guess what? Guess what?'
Betsey danced around the table.

'Go on then – as you're bursting
to tell us!' Mam smiled.

'It's May's birthday on Saturday and she's having a birthday party. I can go, can't I?' Betsey was so excited, she bounced up and down like a tennis ball.

'A party!' said Mam. 'That'll be fun. Of course you can go, Betsey.'

'Yippee! A party!'

Abruptly Betsey stopped dancing. She turned quickly to her mam.

'Can I have a new dress, Mam? And new shoes to go with it? Can I? And a present for May?'

'Betsey, I'm not made of money!' frowned Mam.

'And money doesn't grow on trees,' sniffed Gran'ma Liz.

'Yes it does,' Betsey replied at once.

'Pardon?'

'Money is made of paper and paper comes from trees, so money *does* grow on trees,' said Betsey. 'We did paper at school!'

Mam and Gran'ma Liz looked at each other. Sherena burst out laughing.

'I'll tell you what, Betsey,' said Sherena. 'When you get some money, go and plant it, then wait for a money tree to grow! But make sure you planted the money first!'

'Botheration, Sherena! You're just jealous because I'm going to a party on Saturday and you're not!' said

Betsey. She turned to her mam and Gran'ma Liz. 'When can we buy my new dress and a present for May?'

'As your mam's working, I'll take you shopping tomorrow after school,' said Gran'ma Liz. 'But you can't have all those things.'

'But I want them,' said Betsey. 'I *need* them!'

'You could always not go to May's party,' Gran'ma Liz pointed out.

Betsey opened her mouth to argue, then snapped it shut. She was going to May's party and she'd get a new outfit and a present for May if it was the last thing she did!

The following afternoon, Gran'ma Liz and Betsey headed off to the shops.

'Let's try this store,' said Gran'ma Liz.

They walked in and passed the costume jewellery counter.

'Look!' Betsey tugged at Gran'ma Liz's arm, then pointed.

It was the perfect present. A silver-coloured bracelet with purple stones.

Gran'ma Liz looked at the price tag on the bracelet. 'Hhmm! It's not exactly cheap!' she sniffed.

'But May would love it. Can we get my dress first and then come back?' asked Betsey.

They went to the children's section of the store and walked up and down, up and down the aisles.

'How about this dress?' asked
Gran'ma Liz.

'Nah! Too boring!' Betsey replied.

'What about this one?' Gran'ma
Liz asked.

'Nah! Too long!' said Betsey.

'What's wrong with this one?'

'Too horrible!'

Twenty minutes later, Gran'ma Liz
was getting fed up!

'Betsey, child! My feet are
beginning to hurt,' Gran'ma Liz said.

And then Betsey saw it! It wasn't
exactly a dress. It was a blouse – the
exact same colour of the sea on a sunny
day, with tiny white buttons. And it was
beautiful.

'Can I have that blouse, Gran'ma Liz? It'd look excellent with my white skirt,' said Betsey.

Gran'ma Liz looked at the price tag. She shook her head. 'Betsey, this blouse is too expensive.'

'But I *need* it,' Betsey protested.

'Betsey, if we buy this blouse, there'll barely be enough money over to buy May an ice-cream, let alone the bracelet!' said Gran'ma Liz firmly.

'But . . . but . . .' Betsey protested.

'You can have the bracelet for

May *or* the blouse for yourself. I don't have enough money to buy both.' Gran'ma Liz said. 'Which one do you want? But just remember, it's May's birthday – not your.'

Botheration! Betsey stared at the blouse. She wanted the blouse something fierce. The only trouble was – she wanted the bracelet too! Which one should she choose? She looked across the shop to the costume jewellery counter, then back at her blouse. Gran'ma Liz watched without saying a word.

'I'll . . . I'll have the blouse,' Betsey said at last.

'Are you sure?' said Gran'ma Liz.

Betsey nodded. But inside, she

didn't feel too sure at all . . .

All the way home on the bus, Betsey held on to the carrier bag that had her blouse in it. She kept opening up the bag to look at it. It was so pretty. Betsey didn't even mind that she didn't get new shoes. She'd wear her sandals and *still* look good!

'But what about a present for May . . . ?' said a tiny voice inside Betsey. 'What about May's birthday . . . ?'

'You're very quiet,' said Gran'ma Liz as they got off the bus.

'Gran'ma, do you think I should have bought the bracelet for May instead of the blouse?' Betsey asked.

Gran'ma stroked Betsey's cheek. 'Betsey, it was your decision. What do *you* think you should have done?'

'I don't know,' Betsey replied.

'Then you'll have to work it out for yourself,' shrugged Gran'ma Liz.

And they began to walk home, past the sugar cane fields, past their neighbours' houses with their shady porches. One person even waved at them, but Betsey was too busy to notice.

Later that night, Betsey lay on her side in bed looking at the blouse she'd bought. The sea-blue blouse with white buttons. But the strange thing was, it didn't look as pretty as it did in the shop.

'What about a present for May . . . ?' The voice inside Betsey's head wouldn't leave her alone. It roared like the sea in a September storm. 'A present for May

. . . A present for May . . .' It said.

Betsey put her hands over her ears and turned her back on the blouse. All at once, she didn't even want to look at it any more.

On Thursday Betsey was very quiet and on Friday morning she was quieter still.

'Betsey dear, don't you feel well?' asked Gran'ma Liz.

Betsey shook her head slowly.

'What's the matter, child?' asked Gran'ma Liz.

'I hate that blouse. I hate it! I wish you'd never bought it,' said Betsey.

'You liked it on Wednesday afternoon,' Gran'ma Liz reminded her.

'Well I don't like it now,' said
Betsey.

'Do you want me to take it back
to the store?' asked Gran'ma Liz.

'Could you? *Would you*?' Betsey
asked, hopefully.

'Do you want another blouse
instead?' Gran'ma Liz asked.

Betsey shook her head. 'Can you
buy that bracelet we saw? The bracelet
for May's birthday.'

Gran'ma Liz smiled. 'Are you
sure?'

Betsey nodded.

'Then I'll go and exchange the
blouse today, while you're in school,'
said Gran'ma Liz.

Betsey skipped out of the room.

All at once, she felt a lot better.

The next day at May's party Betsey handed over her present which was now wrapped up. May tore off the wrapping paper and squeaked with delight when she saw the bracelet.

'Oh Betsey, thank you. It's beautiful,' breathed May. 'I'll wear it every day.'

'You look pretty Betsey,' said Ce-Ce. 'I like your top.'

Betsey looked down at her yellow blouse and her white skirt. She smiled up at Gran'ma Liz, then turned to Ce-Ce and said, 'It's not new. I've had this blouse for ages.'

'But you still look pretty,' smiled Gran'ma Liz. 'You've never looked prettier.'

'Look everyone! Look at what Betsey bought me!' May called out.

And Betsey joined the others who were all around May, admiring her new bracelet.

5

Betsey and the Monster Hamburger

"When we get there, I'm going to have a chicken burger,' said Desmond.

'I'm going to have a veggie burger,' said Sherena.

'I'm going to have a hamburger,' said Betsey. 'A big hamburger. The BIGGEST hamburger they've got. A

MONSTER hamburger!'

The whole family was going to
the local burger bar. For once, neither
Mam nor Gran'ma Liz felt like
cooking, so they were all going to eat
out. It was a lovely evening. The air
was warm and a gentle breeze was
blowing.

'I'm going to have a strawberry
milkshake,' said Sherena.

'I think I'll have a vanilla one,' said Desmond.

'I'm going to have two chocolate milkshakes,' said Betsey, skipping down the road.

'Betsey, don't be such a pig,' said Desmond.

'You'll never finish two milkshakes. It takes me ages just to finish one and my stomach is a lot

bigger than yours,' said Sherena.

'I'm going to have two – and you can't stop me,' said Betsey.

'Betsey Biggalow, you will have one milkshake and like it,' Mam called out.

'But Mam, I'm really hungry,' said Betsey.

'One, Betsey,' said Mam firmly. 'You'll have one milkshake or none at all.'

'Botheration!' Betsey muttered under her breath. 'I bet if it was Sherena or Desmond, they could have two if they wanted.'

'Pardon, Betsey?' said Gran'ma Liz.

'Nothing, Gran'ma,' Betsey replied.

Once they reached the burger bar,

Mam asked each of them what they wanted. When it was Betsey's turn, Betsey said, 'I want a MONSTER hamburger and two chocolate milkshakes and a large portion of French fries.'

'Betsey, you'll have a small portion of French fries and one chocolate milkshake,' said Mam.

'But I'm starving.'

'Betsey, your trouble is your eyes are bigger than your stomach. I'm not going to buy all that food for you to leave most of it,' said Mam.

'Can't I at least have the MONSTER hamburger?' sniffed Betsey.

'You'll never finish it,' said Mam.

'I will. I promise,' said Betsey.

'*Please.*'

No, Betsey, you can't . . ." Mam began.

'Please Mam. I will eat it. I'm starving hungry,' said Betsey.

Mam frowned down at Betsey.

'All right then, Betsey,' Mam said at last. 'I'll buy you a MONSTER hamburger and you'd better eat it. I don't want to see any left.'

'You won't,' Betsey beamed.

'Hhmm!' Was all Gran'ma Liz said.

Desmond and Mam went up to the counter to order whilst Gran'ma Liz, Sherena and Betsey found a table. It didn't take long for Mam and

Desmond to join them, each carrying a tray filled with food.

Betsey licked her lips. Her very first MONSTER hamburger! She was going to enjoy this!

Mam put Betsey's MONSTER hamburger in front of her.

'There you are, Betsey,' said Mam.

'Thanks, Mam,' Betsey grinned.

'Eating that will soon wipe the grin off your face, Elizabeth Ruby Biggalow,' said Gran'ma Liz.

'Botheration!' said Betsey.

'Gran'ma, I will finish this hamburger. Just watch.'

'I intend to,' said Gran'ma Liz.

And with that they all started to eat.

Betsey picked up her hamburger with both hands. She looked at it from above, she looked at it from below, she checked each side of it. It was HUGE! In fact it was so big, she hardly knew where to begin.

'Anything wrong, Betsey?' asked Mam.

'No, Mam,' Betsey replied.

Then she opened her eyes W–I–D–E and opened her mouth W–I–D–E–R and bit into her hamburger. Tomato ketchup squirted

out one side of the hamburger and hit
Desmond – PLOOPP! – on the nose.
A dollop of mustard
flew out of the
other side of the
hamburger and
hit Sherena –
SPLATTT! – on
the forehead.

'Betsey, look what you've done.
I look like I've got a nose bleed,' said
Desmond annoyed.

'Betsey chewed and chewed away
at the piece of hamburger she had
managed to bite off. Then she had
some French fries and washed it all
down with some chocolate milkshake.
It was delicious! Betsey took another

bite and another, then another.

The only trouble was, she was beginning to feel full and she hadn't even eaten half of the burger yet. Betsey chewed more and more slowly, as she became more and more full.

'What's the matter, Betsey? Is that hamburger too much for you?' asked Gran'ma Liz.

'Oh no, Gran'ma,' Betsey replied quickly. 'I'm just eating it slowly so that I can remember what every mouthful tastes like.'

Gran'ma Liz and Mam exchanged a look.

'Hhmm!' Was all Gran'ma said.

What am I doing? thought Betsey as she chewed on yet another mouthful. She was stuffed! If she had just one more bite, she would pop like a balloon. But if she stopped now, everyone would say, 'We told you so!'

Then Betsey had an idea. She arranged the paper napkin on her lap to cover her skirt. She broke off a bit of her burger. Then she pretended to put the piece of burger into her mouth but she didn't really . . . Whilst she was pretending to chew, Betsey waited until no one was looking and dropped the little bit of burger from her hand into her napkin. As soon as the coast was clear, Betsey did the same thing again. She broke off a piece and pretended to eat it, but instead dropped it into her napkin. Ten pieces later, there was no more hamburger in her hands – but lots of hamburger sat on the napkin in her lap. Betsey folded up the napkin until none of the hamburger could be seen.

Betsey picked up her chocolate milkshake and took a long drink. Pretending to eat hamburger was very thirsty work!

'Well done, Betsey!' Mam said surprised. 'I must admit, I didn't think you could do it.'

'I told you I was hungry,' said Betsey.

'Your appetite has doubled overnight – and so has your stomach,' said Gran'ma Liz.

'Okay everyone, pass over your

napkins and empty wrappers and cups and I'll put them all on this tray,' said Mam.

Oh no! thought Betsey. She couldn't hand over her napkin to Mam. Her Mam would feel the napkin and immediately guess what was in it. That's when Betsey had another idea.

She deliberately dropped her knife on the floor.

'I'll just pick that up,' said Betsey, and she scooted under the table. Quick like a jack-rabbit, Betsey opened up Sherena's handbag and put in the napkin filled with all the pieces of hamburger. Then she got the knife and sat up again, putting the knife on one of the trays.

'Come on then, everyone. Let's go home,' said Mam. And they all stood up.

On the way home Sherena said, 'Well done, Betsey. I didn't think you'd finish one of those in my life.'

Betsey said nothing. What could she say? And there was just one thing on her mind. How was she going to get the napkin filled with hamburger out of Sherena's bag without anyone finding out.

Botheration! Thought Betsey. Double and triple botheration!

'Sherena, do you want me to carry your handbag?' Betsey asked hopefully.

'What on earth for?' asked Sherena.

'No reason.'

'No, thank you,' said Sherena.

Just at that moment, Betsey felt the back of her neck go all tingly and hot. She turned around and there was Gran'ma Liz standing right behind her. And Gran'ma Liz had that look in her eyes. The look that said, 'Betsey, you're up to something. I don't know what it is, but we both know I'm going to find out!'

And it didn't take her long to find out either! Betsey followed Sherena into the house, hoping for a chance to take her napkin out of Sherena's handbag. But no sooner had they taken just a couple of steps into the house than Prince, the Alsatian dog,

came bounding up to Sherena and
started sniffing at her handbag.

'Prince, what are you doing?'
frowned Sherena.

Prince snatched the handbag and
raced off around the sitting-room with
it. Sherena chased after him, followed
by Betsey and Desmond.

'What's the
matter with that
dog?' asked
Mam.

'I think
I know,' said
Gran'ma Liz.
'Prince, sit! Sit!'
Immediately
Price did as he was told.

'Sherena, bring me your handbag,' said Gran'ma Liz.

Sherena handed over her bag to Gran'ma.

'Now then, Betsey,' said Gran'ma Liz. 'Is there anything you want to say before I open this handbag?'

'Just that I'm sorry and I won't do it again,' Betsey sniffed.

'Hhmm!' said Gran'ma Liz. And she opened the handbag.

'What's going on?' asked Sherena, puzzled.

Gran'ma Liz looked at Betsey. Betsey looked up at Gran'ma Liz. Gran'ma Liz took the napkin out of Sherena's handbag and put it in her cardigan pocket.

'Nothing's going on,' said Gran'ma Liz at last. 'Isn't that right Betsey?'

'That's right, Gran'ma,'said Betsey in a tiny voice.

Betsey couldn't believe it. Gran'ma Liz wasn't going to tell anyone what she'd done!

'Betsey, the next time we go to the burger bar, what are you going to have?' asked Gran'ma Liz.

'One milkshake and a small portion of fries,' Betsey replied.

'No MONSTER hamburger?' asked Sherena.

'I don't care if I never see another hamburger again as long as I live,' said Betsey.

6

The Best Guard Dog in the World

'Oink! Oink! Oink! Oink!'

Betsey snuffled into the kitchen where the whole family was sitting down to breakfast. She snuffled along the ground and oinked again!

'Betsey child, what're you doing?' frowned Gran'ma Liz.

'I'm a pig!' Betsey announced.

'Tell us something we don't already know!' laughed Sherena, Betsey's bigger sister. 'You eat like a pig and thanks to you, our room looks like a pigsty!'

'No, you don't understand. I'm going to spend this weekend being all kinds of animals,' Betsey explained.

'Uh-oh!' said Desmond, Betsey's bigger brother.

'I don't like the sound of that,' said Sherena.

'Sounds like another of Betsey's ideas,' Mam sighed and poured herself another cup of coffee.

Gran'ma Liz just shook her head.

'I know I'm going to be sorry I

asked this, but why d'you want to be all kinds of different animals?' asked Sherena.

'So I can see what it's like of course,' Betsey replied. 'Then I can compare it to being a girl. Mrs Rhodes, my teacher, said that we have to think about which animal we'd most like to be and then say why in class. Well, I can't decide until I've tried to be some of them, can I?'

'Betsey, I'll say one thing for you. You're different!' said Sherena.

'No, I'm not. I'm a pig!' said Betsey. 'Oink! Oink!'

'Betsey, you're getting in everyone's way. Sit down and eat your breakfast,' said Gran'ma Liz.

'Couldn't you put it on the floor for me?' asked Betsey. 'Pigs don't eat at a table with a knife and fork.'

'Elizabeth Ruby Biggalow, you will sit at the table and eat with this family or go without,' said Gran'ma firmly.

Uh-oh! There it was again. Whenever Gran'ma Liz used Betsey's whole, full name, Betsey knew she'd better pay close attention! She stood up at once. Botheration! Being a pig didn't last very long – and she was just getting into it as well! Betsey sat at the table and had a long, hard think.

What animal can I be now? She wondered. Then she had a wonderful idea.

'Sherena, can I borrow your saucer?' Betsey asked.

Puzzled, Sherena lifted up her cup of coffee and handed over the saucer underneath it. Betsey poured some orange juice out of her glass and into the saucer.

'Betsey, what . . .?' But before Sherena could say another word, Betsey bent her head and started lapping at the orange juice.

'Betsey, stop that! And it's going all over the table,' said Gran'ma Liz.

'Miaow!' said Betsey. And she

carried on lapping at her orange juice.

'Elizabeth Ruby Biggalow . . .' Gran'ma said ominously.

Betsey stopped lapping at once. Gran'ma Liz had used her whole, full name *twice* in less than five minutes!

'But Gran'ma, this is how cats drink,' Betsey protested.

'Cats don't drink orange juice,' Desmond pointed out. 'They drink milk.'

'Yeuk!' Betsey's face scrunched up at the thought of it.

'Find some other animal to be,' Gran'ma Liz ordered. 'As a pig you're in the way and as a cat you're too messy.'

And with that Gran'ma Liz

scooped up the saucer and placed it in the sink – so that was the end of that! Betsey sighed and straightened up. It wasn't easy being any kind of animal with Gran'ma Liz around!

Betsey picked up her glass of orange juice and began to drink. Drinking as a cat was much more fun!

After breakfast, when all the dishes had been washed and rinsed and put away, Betsey had another think about what else she could be. She had to become an animal that wasn't in the way and wasn't messy . . .

'Got it!' Betsey said happily.

She went out into the living room and lay down on the floor. She put her hands at her sides and her feet together and started slithering and wriggling.

'Betsey, have you seen my glasses?' Gran'ma Liz walked into the living-room.

'Gran'ma Liz, don't step on me,' Betsey said quickly.

And only just in time too. One more step and Gran'ma Liz would've stepped on Betsey for sure.

Betsey carried on slithering and wriggling.

'What on earth are you doing, child?' Gran'ma Liz asked.

'I'm a worm,' Betsey replied. 'But I'm not making much progress. I've only moved a few centimetres. It must be hard work being a worm. And you almost stepped on me. So it must be quite dangerous being a worm too.'

'It's harder work being your Gran'ma,' said Gran'ma Liz. 'Betsey, get up off the floor. You'll ruin your clothes.'

'But Gran'ma . . .'

'But nothing. Up. NOW!'

With a deep, deep sigh, Betsey stood up. Botheration plus one hundred!

'You're in the way as a pig, you're messy as a cat and your underfoot as a worm!' said Gran'ma Liz. 'I think that's enough animals for one day.'

And so that was that! Botheration plus one million!!

All day long, Betsey racked her brains. What animal could she be that *wouldn't* upset Gran'ma! Maybe she could be a chirp-chirping bird? No Gran'ma would say she was too noisy! Maybe she could be a flying fish – splish-splashing in the bath tub. No. Gran'ma Liz would say she was too wet!

Later that night, as Betsey put on her pyjamas to go to bed, she said to her dog, 'Oh Prince! This is a lot harder than I thought it would be.'

'Woof!' Prince agreed.

As Betsey climbed into bed, she still hadn't decided on which animal she could be.

'I'll think about it in my sleep,' Betsey yawned. 'Then I'm bound to get an answer.'

And with that Betsey pulled the bed clothes up around her neck, closed her eyes and was asleep in less than a minute.

Betsey opened her eyes and was instantly awake. It was the middle of the night. Silvery moonlight streamed in through the window. Betsey sat up and took a look around. Something had woken her up but Betsey wasn't sure what it was. Creak! Creeee–eeeeak! There it was again. Someone was creeping through the house . . .

'Sherena . . . Sherena . . .' Betsey hissed at her sister.

Creeee–eeeak! The strange noise sounded again. Betsey slipped her feet into her slippers and crept towards her sister's bed.

'Sherena . . .'

But Sherena wasn't there . . . Betsey knew what had happened at once.

'Prince! Prince!' Betsey whispered to the dog lying beside her bed.

'Wake up! There are kidnappers in the house. And they've got Sherena!'

But Prince refused to budge. He lay beside Betsey's bed, his eyes tight shut. Betsey's heart pounded like a sledge hammer as she tip-toed to the bedroom door. She was terrified. There were kidnappers in the house. Betsey had to get to Mam *and* Gran'ma Liz. But how could she do it? She looked back at Prince.

Huh! Some guard dog you are! Betsey thought with disgust.

Guard dog . . . That was it! Betsey thought of a way to wake up Mam and Gran'ma Liz without the kidnappers getting to her first. Betsey opened her bedroom door and got down on all fours so that the kidnappers wouldn't spot her.

'WOOF! WOOF!' Betsey barked at the top of her voice. 'WOOF! WOOF! WOOF!'

Then everything happened at once. There was a bang and a crash in the living-room, followed by the lights being switched on in Mam's and Gran'ma Liz's bedrooms.

'WOOF! WOOF!' Betsey barked even louder. Her throat was getting sore but she wasn't going to stop now. At long last Price joined in, but Betsey was even louder.

'What on earth is going on?' Gran'ma Liz came out into the living-room and switched on the light.

There lay Sherena, sprawled out

on the floor. And next to her was a puddle of spilt orange juice, an empty plate and chocolate biscuits scattered here, there and everywhere.

'Sherena, what d'you think you're doing,' Mam frowned.

'I was hungry so I decided to have a snack,' Sherena sat up. 'But when Betsey started making all that noise, it startled me and I tripped over.'

'You wanted a snack at three o'clock in the morning?' Mam said crossly. 'Sherena, you can clean up that mess and go straight back to bed.'

'Betsey, was it you making that racket?' asked Gran'ma Liz.

'I thought Sherena was being kidnapped,' said Betsey. 'And I wanted to wake up you and Mam without the kidnappers getting me! So I decided to be a guard dog!'

'Well, you woke us up, all right,' said Gran'ma Liz. 'I should think you've woken up the whole street as well!'

'I make an excellent guard dog,' Betsey decided. 'I know! That's what I'll be in class on Monday – the best guard dog in the world.'

'Betsey, I prefer you as a girl,' sniffed Sherena. 'Then I wouldn't have got caught and I could've had a snack in peace!'

'Betsey, you can be a guard dog any time you like,' smiled Mam. 'I feel very safe knowing that you're in the house!'

Betsey Moves House

'Betsey, go and tidy your bedroom,'
Gran'ma Liz commanded.

'It's Sherena's turn,' said Betsey.

'No, it isn't. I did it yesterday.
It's your turn today,' Sherena argued.

'But I wanted to play with May.
We were going to play Robin Hood

with my new bow and arrows,' Betsey said. 'Sherena, couldn't you do it for me . . . ?'

'Betsey . . .' Gran'ma Liz's voice held a warning.

'Oh, all right,' said Betsey reluctantly. And off she went to tidy her room.

Ages later, when Betsey had finished, Gran'ma Liz said, 'Betsey it's your turn to help me with the washing-up.'

'It's Desmond's turn,' Betsey protested.

'Oh no, it isn't. It's my turn tomorrow. It's your turn today,' Desmond said.

'Oh but . . .' Betsey began.

'Betsey—' There it was again –
that warning note in Gran'ma's voice.

'It's not fair. It's just not fair,'
Betsey muttered under her breath. 'If
I had my own house, I could do what
I liked when I liked and no one could
boss my head.'

'Did you say something, child?'
asked Gran'ma Liz.

'No, Gran'ma,' Betsey answered
at once. And she followed Gran'ma
into the kitchen to help with the
washing-up.

When Betsey had finished, May
came round. But by then Betsey was
in a bad mood.

'What's the matter with you?'
May asked.

'I'm fed up!' That's what's the matter,' Betsey said. 'I wish I had my own house and no one to tell me what to do!'

And that's when Betsey had her extra brilliant idea. It was such an exciting idea that Betsey couldn't help hopping up and down. Betsey took May by the hand and pulled her into the kitchen where Gran'ma Liz was reading her newspaper.

'Gran'ma Liz,' Betsey began, 'can I make a house in the backyard?'

'Pardon?!' Gran'ma Liz stared at Betsey.

'Can I make myself a house – a very small house – in the backyard?' Betsey repeated. 'May will help me, won't you?'

'Sure! But how do we do it?'
May asked.

Gran'ma Liz sat back in her
chair. 'I'd like to hear that too,' she
said.

'I'll make it with branches and
leaves,' Betsey announced. 'I saw how
it was done on the telly last week. I'll
make myself a hut and then I can live
there and have my own room and
Sherena will have to tidy up her
bedroom all by herself. Can I,
Gran'ma? Please! *Please*!'

'Go on then,' Gran'ma Liz
smiled. 'Just don't make a mess in *this*
house.'

Betsey skipped out to the

backyard, followed by May. She was going to do it. She was going to make her very own house!

'Betsey, we can't make a hut. It'll be too difficult,' said May.

'Not if we get some help,' smiled Betsey, and she pointed to her brother who was at the far end of the backyard with a drawing pad and a pencil in his hands. Betsey and May ran over to him.

'What're you doing?' asked Betsey.

'Drawing some chickens for a school project!' said Desmond. 'I just wish they'd keep still.'

'Desmond, I want to make a hut – right here in the middle of the backyard,' Betsey beamed. 'Will you help me?'

'Why d'you want to do that?' Desmond asked. 'And why should I help you?'

'Because I'll live in the hut instead of the house and then none of you can tell me what to do,' said Betsey.

'Well, if it'll get you out of the house, then I'll definitely help you,' Desmond said at once. 'We'll need long branches and banana leaves and palm fronds and lots of string.'

'I'll get the leaves,' said May.

'I'll get the string,' said Betsey and she dashed into the house.

Ten minutes later, they all gathered in the backyard again.

Desmond showed them how to set up the branches with leaves and fronds to make the walls. Then they each took long lengths of string and tied the leaves and fronds on to the branches.

It was very hard, hot work but as last it was all finished. They all stepped back to admire the hut.

'It looks wonderful,' breathed Betsey. 'Just like a real house.'

'It's not bad at all,' Desmond admitted.

'Desmond, you can't come in,' said Betsey. 'Not unless I say so, 'cause it's my house.'

'Thanks a lot!' sniffed Desmond. 'Anyway, I've got homework to do, so you keep your house.' And with that,

off Desmond
marched.

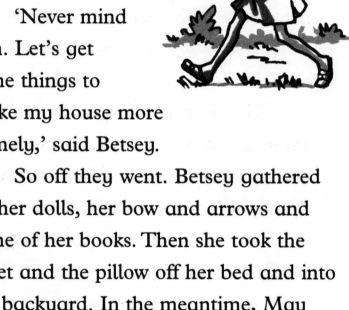

'That was a
bit mean, Betsey,'
said May.

'Never mind
him. Let's get
some things to
make my house more
homely,' said Betsey.

So off they went. Betsey gathered
up her dolls, her bow and arrows and
some of her books. Then she took the
sheet and the pillow off her bed and into
the backyard. In the meantime, May
made some ham and tomato
sandwiches.

'It's a bit cramped,' said May, once

everything was placed in the hut.

'That doesn't matter,' smiled Betsey. 'It's lovely and it's *mine*!'

They sat down to eat their sandwiches but the hut was so small they were squashed up against each other and their feet stuck out of the entrance.

'Shall we play a game?' May suggested after they'd finished eating.

'No, it'll make my new house untidy.' Betsey shook her head.

'Your house is too small to get untidy,' said May.

'You're the only one making my house untidy. And if you don't like my house you can always leave,' said Betsey, crossly.

'I don't mind if I do.' May crawled out of the hut and stood. 'I won't stay where I'm not wanted.'

Betsey folded her arms as she sat in her house, getting crosser than cross. This was her house and she wasn't going to let May or Desmond

in it, or anyone else for that matter. She was going to keep it all for herself. And that way it would stay clean and tidy and be all hers. Betsey looked around her house. It was small but perfect. She couldn't believe she had
her very own home. The only trouble was . . . it was a bit lonely. There was no one to play with and no one to talk to.

'That doesn't matter,' Betsey told herself.

But as she sat in her home, all alone, she began to feel that it did. What was the point of having her very own house if she didn't have anyone to share it with. The backyard was so quiet. She could hear the bamboo plants at the side of the yard, creaking as the wind blew

through them but that was all. She
missed Gran'ma's laugh and Mam's
voice. She missed Sherena's moaning
and complaining. She missed May's
company. She even missed Desmond
teasing her. Betsey stuck her head out of
the entrance to her hut. Grey clouds
were scudding across the sky. Betsey
crawled out of the hut and stood up in
the backyard. She smiled up at the sky,
then went into the main house. The
whole family, as well as May, was sitting
in the living-room, watching telly.

'What are you doing here?' asked
Desmond.

'I thought you had your own home
now,' said Gran'ma Liz.

'I do, but it's going to rain and my

house isn't waterproof,' said Betsey.

And sure enough, the moment she'd said that there came a flash of lightning and a clap of thunder. Giant raindrops hammered on the roof and the windows.

'See!' said Betsey, happily. 'I told you it was going to rain.'

'Quick, Betsey. Your house is going to be washed away,' said Desmond, jumping up. 'Come on. If we act now we can save it.'

Betsey shook her head. 'No, it's okay Desmond. That wasn't my real home. My real home is where my family and friends are.'

'Betsey, that's a lovely thing to say,' smiled Gran'ma Liz.

'And MAY, I'm sorry I was so mean about my house, you can come in any time you want to.'

'Are you going to make another one?' asked May.

'I might do,' said Betsey. 'But next time, I'll make it big enough for *everyone*!'

And just to show she meant it, Betsey gave everyone a hug – even the dog, Prince.

8

Betsey and the Soft Landing

'Sherena, can I ride your bicycle?
Please, *please*?'

'No, Betsey,' Sherena replied.
'It's too big for you. You'd never get
your feet on the pedals anyway.'

'I would if you helped me,'
Betsey said.

'No,' said Sherena firmly. 'You're only used to four-wheel bikes.'

'No, I'm not. I've ridden on May's bike and that's only got two wheels. Please Sherena.'

'My bike is a lot bigger than May's' said Sherena.

'But I want some exercise,' Betsey tried.

'Go for a walk then,' said Sherena.

'But Sherena . . .' Betsey began.

'Betsey, I said no and I mean no,' said Sherena. 'I didn't save all my money for over two years and work every weekend and completely remake a second-hand bike just so you could wreck it for me.'

'Botheration Sherena! You're so

mean,' said Betsey, crossly.

'And you're such a pest,' replied Sherena. And off she walked.

Betsey went out into the front yard. There was Sherena's bike, lying on it's side – and Betsey wanted to ride on it. She wanted to ride on it something fierce! Oh, to ride with the wind on her face and the pedals racing round, going fast, fast, *fast*. Betsey walked over to the bike. She lifted it up, holding on to the handlebars. Maybe if she sat on it . . . Just for a minute. Just for a moment.

'Oh, if only I had a bike of my own . . .' Betsey whispered. Then she could ride and ride – all the way across Barbados and back!

Betsey leaned
the bike towards
her, her hands on
the handlebars.
She squeezed the
brakes. The bike
felt *wonderful*.

'I'll just have a
quick sit on it,' Betsey
decided. After all,
one teeny, tiny sit wouldn't hurt.
Betsey began to swing her right leg
over the bike.

'Betsey Biggalow! I hope you're
not thinking of riding that thing.'
Gran'ma Liz appeared from nowhere
to stand on the front porch.

'No, Gran'ma Liz,' said Betsey

quickly. 'Of course not.'

Betsey hopped off the bike.

'I should think not,' said
Gran'ma. 'I've told you this before. If
the good Lord had meant for us to go
tearing around to up, down, below
and above on a bicycle, then we would
have wheels instead of legs.'

Gran'ma Liz didn't even approve
of bikes.

'Come on in, child,' said
Gran'ma. 'You haven't finished all
your chores yet.'

So Betsey went inside the house.
But for the rest of the day, everything
Betsey saw reminded her of Sherena's
bike. Round things like plug holes, the
record player turntable and the tops of

tins all reminded her of wheels on her sister's bike. When Betsey sat down, she wondered if the saddle of Sherena's bike was as firm, as comfortable.

Finally Betsey could stand it no more.

'Botheration!' Betsey muttered to herself. 'I want to ride that bike and I'm going to ride that bike!'

After dinner, Betsey went out into the front yard. The bike was still there, lying on the ground. Betsey picked it up and stroked it.

'If you were my bike, I'd look after you better than this,' Betsey whispered.

'Hi, Betsey. What are you doing? Talking to your sister's bike?' Betsey's good friend May appeared, making Betsey jump.

'May . . .' Betsey put her finger over her lips, 'don't tell anyone but I'm off for a ride.'

'You can't.' May stared. 'Sherena's bike is much too big for you. You'll fall off and break every bone in your body!'

'How many times have you ridden on it?' May asked.

'Er . . . this will be the first time,' Betsey admitted. 'But it can't be much more difficult than riding your bike. You just sit on the saddle and hold on the handlebars and pedal.'

'Betsey . . .' May began.

'Botheration, May, are you going to help me or not?' asked Betsey.

'Oh, all right then,' May said at last. 'But be careful.'

'You can be my lookout. Tell me if anyone's coming.' Betsey swung her leg over the bike. She grinned at May.

'Here I go!' laughed Betsey and she jumped up to sit on the saddle, her feet on the pedals.

The bike wibbled and wobbled while Betsey tried to steady it.

'I'm doing it! I'm riding!' Betsey squealed with delight. 'And Sherena said my feet wouldn't reach the pedals! My sister doesn't know what she's talking about.'

'Hush up!' May warned, looking around.

'I'm going to ride down the footpath to the beach and back,' said Betsey. And off she went, pedalling furiously.

'Betsey, no! COME BACK!' May called after her.

Betsey hardly heard her friend. The warm wind was on her face and the pedals were racing round and round. It was even more fun than Betsey had thought it would be.

'What's all the shouting about?' Sherena came out of the house. Then she saw Betsey – and her bike – disappearing into the distance. 'My bike! Betsey! I told you that you couldn't ride it. Just wait till I catch you,' Sherena yelled.

Betsey turned her head to look at her sister. That was a big, BIG mistake! The bike started to wobble and to wibble even more than before. Betsey squeezed the brakes. The bike started to slow down, but then Betsey realised something. Her legs *were* long enough to reach the pedals, but they *weren't* long enough to reach the ground. Sitting on the saddle meant that she could only reach the pedals. How was she going to stop the bike without falling on the hard ground and hurting herself?

'Sherena! May! HELP!' Betsey shouted.

'Hang on, Betsey!' Sherena raced after her sister.

'We're coming.' May dashed after Sherena.

Betsey stuck her legs out straight in front of her, but she didn't dare squeeze the brakes very hard. Now Betsey was on the beach. Sand flew everywhere. And she was heading for the sea.

'I don't want to get wet!' Betsey shrieked. She decided she'd rather fall on the sand than in the sea, so she pressed the brakes – hard!

Too hard. Betsey went flying over the handlebars and both she and the bike fell – SPLOOSH! – into the water. The bike lay on it's side, the back wheel spinning around. Betsey sat in the water, shaking her head and wondering what had happened. She was sitting in only a few centimetres of water but it was wet and felt yukky! Sherena and May came running up.

'Betsey, are you all right?' Sherena asked anxiously.

Betsey stood up, her shirt and trousers soaked. 'I . . . I think so,'

she said.

'Well, you won't be when I've finished with you,' Sherena said angrily. 'I thought I told you not to ride on my bike.'

'Don't worry, Sherena.' Betsey shook her head. 'I'm not even going to sit on it again until my legs grow at least another ten centimetres!'

Sherena made Betsey pick up the bike and *push* it all the way back to the house.

'And when we get home, you can dry it and clean it and oil it too,' said Sherena.

And for once Betsey didn't argue.

'Never mind, Betsey,' whispered May. 'You didn't break every bone in your body like I thought you would!'

'The sea gave me a nice, soft landing,' Betsey whispered back. 'It's just a shame my landing was so wet as well!'

Betsey's
Bad Day!

The moment Betsey opened her eyes, she was awake. She grinned and sat up. Saturday morning! And only one more week until Dad came home. And no school! *And* they were all going into town today. Today was going to be a good day!

'Yippee! Saturday!' Betsey sprang out of bed.

She put on her slippers and went to have her wash. When she'd finished, she went for her breakfast. Sherena and Desmond were already at the table. So was Gran'ma Liz.

'Sit down, Betsey,' said Mam. 'I'll get your breakfast.'

Betsey turned in her chair to look at Mam.

'What's for breakfast, Mam?' Betsey sniffed the air. 'Ham?'

'And scrambled eggs,' said Mam.

'Scrumptious,' grinned Betsey. She turned around. There before her was a long, cool glass of orange juice.

'Yumptious-scrumptious!' said

Betsey. And she picked up the glass and started to drink. Oh, it was cold! Oh, it was refreshing! Oh, it was delicious!

'Betsey, you toad! That's *my* orange juice,' said Desmond.

'Then what's it doing in front of my plate?' Betsey replied.

'I don't know and I don't care,' said Desmond. 'It's still my orange juice.'

'Desmond boy, don't call your

sister a toad,' said Gran'ma Liz. 'If she's a toad, then you must be one too 'cause you're her brother.' Desmond started to sulk.

'Desmond, there's plenty of orange juice for everyone, so behave,' said Mam. 'And Betsey, if you want some orange juice, pour some for yourself. Don't just help yourself to your brother's.'

'But . . but . . .' Betsey protested. Botheration! The glass *had* been in front of her plate. Never mind, today was *Saturday*! Betsey handed over her now half empty glass to Desmond.

'Huh!' said Desmond, still sulking. He put the glass to his lips and finished his orange juice with one gulp. Then he poured himself another one.

'Pass the sugar, Betsey,' said Sherena, stirring her coffee.

'Manners!' said Gran'ma Liz. 'What do you say?'

'Please,' said Sherena. 'Please, please, please!'

With a grin, Betsey handed over the sugar bowl. Sherena added a spoonful of sugar to her coffee, then another spoonful, then another, and another.

'Sherena girl, by the time you're sixteen, you'll not have one tooth left in your head if you carry on like that,' said Gran'ma Liz.

'I like it sweet, Gran'ma Liz,'

smiled Sherena. 'Besides, I want to put on weight. I'm skinny as a needle – worse luck. Everyone says so.' Sherena lifted her coffee cup to her lips. She'd barely taken one sip when immediately she started to gag and cough. The cup fell from her hand. Both hands flew to her throat, as she coughed and spluttered and coughed some more, her eyes watering.

'Sherena? Sherena, what's the matter?' Mam ran over to her and so did Gran'ma Liz. Betsey sprang out of her chair. 'Sherena, are you all right?'

'Salt!' Sherena coughed. 'There's s-salt in that bowl, not s-sugar.'

'Whose turn was it to fill the sugar bowl last night?' Mam frowned.

All eyes turned slowly to Betsey. Betsey's mouth dropped open.

'I thought I put sugar in it – honest!' she said quickly. Mam took the sugar bag and the salt bag out of the cupboard.

'Which bag did you use?' she asked.

Betsey stared at the bags. One was white and red, the other was red all over. The first bag said SALT on it and the second bag said FINEST SUGAR.

'Er . . . I . . . er . . .' began
Betsey.

'I'm waiting, Betsey.' Mam
pursed her lips.

'I used the white and red bag to
fill the sugar bowl,' Betsey admitted,
adding quickly. 'But it wasn't my
fault. The salt bag was on the kitchen
table and I thought it was the sugar
bag and I was in a hurry because I
was missing the film on the T.V. . .'

'More haste, less speed.'
Gran'ma Liz wagged her finger.

Mam frowned. 'Betsey! What is
the matter with you today? First you
drink your brother's orange juice, then
you try and poison your sister.'

'But it wasn't purpose work,' said

Betsey. 'It wasn't deliberate. I only . . .'

'Betsey, if you carry on like this, we'll leave you with May's parents and go to town without you,' said Mam. 'If I take you into town, goodness only knows what havoc you'll cause.'

'I won't cause any havoc, Mam. I promise,' Betsey said quickly. She didn't want to miss the trip into town. No, she didn't!

'So you say,' said Mam. 'But you've only been awake for two seconds and look what's happened already.'

Betsey couldn't argue with that so she said nothing. She thought a lot though. And her thoughts started with 'botheration' and ended with 'botheration'!

At least it's Saturday – and only seven more days till Dad comes home, Betsey thought to herself. That thought cheered her up a little.

After breakfast, they all had to hurry up and get ready in order to catch the bus into town. In her bedroom, Betsey kicked off her slippers and looked around for the pink and grey trainers her mam had bought her. She found one by the bedroom door where she and Sherena always left their shoes but could she find the other one? No, she couldn't! Betsey searched high and low, under the bed and in the bottom of the wardrobe.

'Betsey! Speed up!' Mam called out.

'Coming, Mam,' Betsey called back. Betsey hunted to the left of the bedroom and to the right of the bedroom and she still couldn't find her other trainer.

'BETSEY!' Mam said. 'What are you doing? We're going to miss our bus.'

'Mam, I can't find one of my trainers,' Betsey yelled.

'Then wear your sandals, but hurry up! That bus won't wait forever.'

Betsey stood in the middle of the room, her hands on her hips. Botheration! Double botheration! Where was that other trainer?

'Betsey!' Mam came into the room. 'Come on.'

'But Mam, I wanted to wear my trainers,' Betsey said.

Mam looked around the room. She pointed to under the bureau. 'Isn't that your other shoe?'

Betsey looked down. There, just sticking out from the bottom of the chest of drawers was the other trainer.

'But Mam, I didn't put my trainer there . . .' Betsey said, puzzled.

'It didn't crawl under there by itself, Betsey. What has got into you this morning?' Mam sighed. 'Now, put on your trainer and let's go.'

At last they left the house. Desmond walked with Gran'ma Liz and Sherena walked with Mam. Betsey walked by herself behind everyone else. They were all talking and laughing. Everyone except Betsey.

'I might as well call today My-Bad-Day instead of Saturday,' Betsey muttered to herself. 'Seems like everything I touch is going wrong and nothing I do is going right.'

Betsey sighed and sighed some

more. Gran'ma Liz turned around.

'Betsey, we're off to town,' smiled Gran'ma Liz. 'So put your face straight before the wind changes direction and you face is stuck with that gloomy look on it. We'll get our provisions and when we've finished we can all go for an ice-cream.'

Ice-cream! Scrumptious! Double scrumptious! That was more like it!

The bus came along and juddered to a halt just as they reached the bus stop.

'Jump up! Jump up!' laughed Gran'ma Liz. 'We're off to town!'

And they all scrambled aboard. Soon they'd reached the market in town.

The town was even busier and

better than Betsey remembered. They didn't come to town too often as there were plenty of small shops locally. But about once a month, they all climbed aboard a bus and went shopping for the provisions they couldn't buy from the local shops. Betsey sniffed the air. She could smell plantain cooking and fried fish and all different kinds of fruit like freshly picked bananas and mangoes and paw-paws and coconuts. Yumptious-scrumptious!

Betsey grinned. Saturday felt better already. Then Betsey saw something that made her eyes open wide as plates and made her mouth drop open and made her heart beat faster then fast. There, across the

street. Dad!

'Dad! DAD!' Betsey yelled out.

Dad heard Betsey's voice and turned. He grinned and waved once the road was clear, ran across it. Dad! There followed such huggings and cuddlings.

'I wasn't expecting you for another week.' Mam smiled happily.

'My last exam wasn't meant to be until the end of next week but they brought it forward so I've finished my exams now.' Dad grinned. 'I decided not to tell you all but to surprise you. My plane landed about an hour ago.'

'Are you a doctor yet?' Betsey asked eagerly.

'Not yet, Betsey.' Dad shook his

head. 'I've got one more year of studying to do first.'

'So how long are you going to be home for?' asked Gran'ma Liz.

'A few weeks.' Dad grinned. 'The exams are over and I'm on holiday.'

'Yippee!' Sherena and Desmond shouted.

'I knew it.' Betsey smiled. 'I knew today was going to be a good day!'

And she was right.

10

Betsey on the Telly

Betsey moved closer to the telly.

'Betsey child, you'll ruin your eyes if you sit that close to the TV screen,' said Gran'ma Liz.

Betsey got up and stood in front of everyone.

'Betsey, move! I can't see,'

Sherena complained.

'I've decided I want to be on the telly,' Betsey announced.

'Oh dear . . .'

'Another one of Betsey's ideas!' Groans and sighs and shakes of the head filled the living-room!

'I'm serious. I want to be on there.' Betsey pointed to the TV screen. 'Gran'ma Liz, how do I get on the telly?'

'The only way you'll ever be on the telly is if you sit on it!' Desmond said before Gran'ma could reply.

'Desmond, behave!' said Gran'ma Liz, laughing.

'I mean it,' said Betsey, crossly. 'I want to be on the TV.

'Betsey, I'd much rather see you in the flesh than on TV. Now come and sit next to me so we can all see the screen.'

'But Gran'ma . . .'

'Betsey, I have no idea how you'd go about getting on the TV. You'll have to become an actress or go into politics or read the news or something like that,' said Gran'ma Liz.

'Hhmm!' Betsey sat down next to Gran'ma but she wasn't watching the evening film any more. She was thinking hard. Betsey didn't know how yet but she *was* going to do it. One way or another she was going to be on the telly.

Betsey had a plan for the next

market day. This time she Betsey wasn't as excited about it as she was far too busy trying to work out how to get on the TV. The market was full of hustle and bustle but Betsey hardly noticed any of it.

'Betsey, are you all right? You're very quiet,' said Desmond.

'Too quiet,' Sherena agreed.

'I'm fine,' Betsey said, still deep in thought.

Gran'ma Liz looked at Betsey very carefully but she didn't say a word. Instead she led the way to the fish stall first. Betsey loved the smell of fish – salt fish, flying fish, crab, snapper . . . But not today. Betsey was still too busy trying to work out her problem.

And then she saw the answer! Over by the bread and cake stall was a thin man with a camcorder. The man moved the camcorder this way and that, filming the whole market. Betsey's eyes opened wider than wide. That man was filming! Maybe his film would be on the telly . . .

Betsey raced over to him and started jumping up and down in front of him.

'Betsey, what on earth are you doing?

And don't run off like that,' panted
Gran'ma when she reached Betsey.

'I'm going to be on the TV,'
Betsey said proudly. And she carried
on jumping up and down.

The thin man lowered his
camcorder. 'Er . . . I sorry, dear, but
I'm just filming my holiday. I'm going
to show all my friends back in England
how wonderful this market is.'

Betsey stopped jumping. 'You're
not making a programme for the
telly?' she said, disappointed.

'I'm afraid not.' The thin man
shook his head. 'Sorry!'

Gran'ma Liz led the way back to
the others, warning Betsey not to run
off in case she got lost. As Betsey's

family carried on through the market,
Betsey felt a bit let down.

'No!' Betsey muttered firmly.
'I'm not going to give up. Not yet at
any rate.'

And then she saw what she was
looking for! A tall woman was holding a
big microphone in her hand and talking

to a stallholder in the market. Betsey grabbed hold of Gran'ma Liz's hand and rushed over to the tall woman.

'Hello! My name is Betsey Biggalow. Are you making a TV programme?' asked Betsey, hopefully.

The tall woman frowned down at Betsey. 'No, I'm making a programme for the radio.'

Betsey sighed. That wasn't the same thing at all!

'Betsey, come away. We've got shopping to buy,' said Gran'ma Liz. 'And please don't drag me all over the market.'

The rest of the morning was spent buying provisions. Betsey looked up and down and back and forth, but no one looked like they were making a TV programme, so that when at last it was time to go home, Betsey wanted to cry. She was going to get on the telly or *burst*.

As they walked up the road from the bus stop, Betsey lagged behind, trying to think of a way of getting on the telly.

'Look! Dad's got something!' Desmond shouted.

With those words, Betsey forgot everything else and charged up the road. There was Dad, standing on the steps outside the front door. And he was holding something strange . . . Only when Betsey reached him did she realise what it was. Dad was holding a camcorder. Betsey was so surprised, her mouth fell open and she stared at Dad.

'Come on, Betsey. I'm filming you so do something!' Dad laughed.

'Where did you get the camera from?' asked Desmond.

'I hired it for the day,' explained Dad. 'I'm going to film the whole family. That way I'll have a recording of all of you when I have to go away again. I can watch the DVD on my TV every day to see all of you and hear your voices.'

Betsey hopped up and down with joy. It wasn't going to happen *exactly* as she'd planned but not only was she going to be on the TV, she was going to be on DVD as well!

Dad filmed the whole family as they entered the house, all bubbling with laughter and chatting.

'Act normally!' said Dad.

And everyone did – except Betsey. She was too busy hogging the camera. It didn't matter which way Dad turned, Betsey was in front of him!

'Betsey, let other people get a look in!' said Sherena.

Dad spent the whole day filming – first Mam and Gran'ma Liz, then Sherena and Desmond and finally it was Betsey's turn.

'What d'you want me to do, Dad?' Betsey asked.

'Anything you like,' said Dad, pointing the camcorder at Betsey. 'You can sing or dance or say something.'

Betsey had a quick think. 'I'll say something,' she decided. 'Dad, I'll be glad when you're a doctor and can come home for good – but I'm glad you're not one yet so you had to make this recording!'

Dad laughed.

'I wanted to be on the telly and thanks to you, I'm going to do it.' Betsey walked over to Dad and gave him a great, big kiss.

'You're welcome, sweet pea!' Dad smiled. 'Okay everyone, it's time to see the results.'

Everyone sat down to see what Dad had come up with. Dad plugged the camcorder into the telly and started it up. The TV screen cleared and there was Mam sitting in the living-room. And who was that creeping into the picture to sit at Mam's feet? Betsey! Mam smiled and waved at the camera and said how much she missed Dad when he was away. Then it was Gran'ma Liz's turn.

Gran'ma Liz was in the kitchen singing. She didn't realise Dad was filming her at first. When she did, she tried to shoo Dad away. But who was standing right beside her as she tried to stop Dad from filming her? Betsey! And who was that dancing behind Sherena and Desmond as they waved to the camera? Betsey. Betsey was everywhere!

'It's like watching the Betsey Biggalow show!' Sherena complained.

'Well, I did say I'd be on the telly,'

Betsey pointed out. 'I just didn't realise how talented and brilliant I'd be!'

'You're a star, Betsey!' laughed Dad. And no one could argue with that!

MALORIE BLACKMAN

Malorie Blackman has shot to fame since she published her first book in 1990. Many prizes have come her way including the WHSmith Mind Boggling Award for HACKER, the Children's Book Award for her brilliant novel NOUGHTS AND CROSSES (and it's sequels), and has been shortlisted for the Carnegie Prize. Several of Malorie's books have been very successfully televised and also been big hits as stage productions.

A former computer database manager, Malorie lives in South London with her husband and daughter, and plays music in her spare time.

MALORIE BLACKMAN

THE BIG BOOK OF BETSEY BIGGALOW

Illustrated by Juliet Percival

Ten more funny, warm stories with this lovable young miss who knows her own mind, but doesn't always get what she wants!

"Malorie Blackman is an author with enormous appeal for young readers and a sure sense of what will captivate and delight them."

Linda Newbery

ISBN 978-1-903-014-69-8 • £6.99 • PAPERBACK

If you've enjoyed this book, you can find
more great titles from Barn Owl at

www.barnowlbooks.com

Barn Owl Books would like to thank, most profoundly, the following people, both friends and colleagues, who have generously made donations to the

BARN OWL APPEAL

The fund exists to keep Barn Owl publishing books and flying high in the literary skies, bringing the best of past writing into the present.

Marianne Adey

Pat Almond

Rachel Anderson

Lynne Reid Banks

Steve Barlow

Clive Barnes

Malorie Blackman

David Bradby

Theresa Breslin

Irene Breugel

Katie Brown

Louise Brown

Natasha Brown

Sarah Butler

Carousel Magazine

Jo Christian

Fred Crawley

Gillian Cross

Finette Deverell

Chris D'Lacey

Ruth & Derek Foxman

Frances Lincoln Publishers

Morag Fraser

Adele Geras

Nicola Gordon

Jim Gordon

Catherine Gordon

Lindsay Gordon

Andrew Gordon

Graham-Cameron
– illustators

Mary Green

Dennis Hamley

Kathy Henderson

Susan Himmelweit

Nigel Hinton

Mary Hoffman

Clodagh Howes

Julia Jarman

Mary & Bill Kennedy

David Kleinman

Richard Kuper

Liz Laird

Marilyn Malin

Anne Mallinson

Kara May

John McLay

David Metz

Gill Moorhouse

Michael Morpurgo

Beverley Naidoo

Linda Newbery

Jane Nissen

Linda Owen Lloyd

Kate Petty

Frank Rogers

Prof. Kim Reynolds

Hannah Sackett

Marsha Saunders

Susan Schonfield

Steve Skidmore

Angela Smith

Jeremy Strong

Howard Stirrup

Pat Thompson

Monica Threlfall

Elinor Updale

Peter Usborne

Miss A Walker

Bob Wilson

Dame Jacqueline Wilson

For information about Barn Owl Books or to make a donation please visit

www.barnowlbooks.com